POKÉMON™

THE SERIES

SUN & MOON

Go, Popplio!

Adapted by Maria S. Barbo

©2017 The Pokémon Company International. ©1997-2017 Nintendo,
Creatures, GAME FREAK, TV Tokyo, ShoPro, JR Kikaku.™, ® Nintendo.

Published by Scholastic Inc., *Publishers since 1920.* SCHOLASTIC
and associated logos are trademarks and/or registered trademarks
of Scholastic Inc.

The publisher does not have any control over and does not assume any
responsibility for author or third-party websites or their content.

This book is a work of fiction. Names, characters, places, and incidents are either the product of the author's
imagination or are used fictitiously, and any resemblance to actual persons, living or dead, business
establishments, events, or locales is entirely coincidental.

ISBN 978-1-338-14866-4

10 9 8 7 6 5 4 3 2 1   17 18 19 20 21

Printed in the U.S.A.   40

First printing 2017

SCHOLASTIC INC.

"Let's try again, Popplio," said Ash's friend Lana.

The two Trainers were on the beach with their Pokémon.

Lana's Popplio took a deep breath.

Then it blew a water balloon.

"Awesome!" said Ash.

"You're doing great, Popplio!" said Lana.

"Not possible," said Ash's Rotom Dex.

"That water balloon is one hundred fifty percent bigger than normal!"

"Wow! Go, go!" Ash pumped a fist in the air.

"Two hundred percent," Rotom Dex declared. "Two hundred fifty percent . . ."

The balloon was bigger than Ash and Pikachu!

"*Pika?*" Pikachu backed away.

The balloon shook. Then . . .

Pop! The balloon burst!

Water splashed down on Pikachu and Ash.

"We will keep trying," said Lana. "Soon we can ride in a balloon."

"What do you mean?" Ash asked.

"It's my dream to ride a big balloon all over the ocean," Lana said. "Then I can find deepwater Pokémon no one has ever seen!"

"Sounds great!" said Ash.

Ash and Pikachu were studying at the Pokémon School in Alola.

They had made a lot of friends there.

Their new friend Lana knew all about Water-type Pokémon.

"Okay, class!" said Professor Kukui. "Today's field trip is about getting to know marine Pokémon. Lana will be our teacher."

"Lapras and Wailmer will take us to a great fishing spot," Lana said.

"Those must be Ride Pokémon," said
James.

Team Rocket was spying on Ash—*again.*
They hoped to steal Pikachu.

"And that one's for me!" Jessie pointed at
Lana's Lapras.

"Ding, ding!" said Meowth. "I just got a brain flash! We'll steal that Pokémon and escape out to sea. Then Team Rocket will be . . ."

"Leaders of the sea!" Jessie and James shouted.

"There are lots of marine Pokémon in this spot," Lana told Ash.

Ash cast his lure into the sea.

He waited, but nothing bit. Not even Magikarp.

"Let's keep trying," he told Pikachu.

Pikachu dipped its tail into the sea.
"*Pika?*" Something tugged. It had a bite!
"*Pika! Pika!*" it called to Ash.
Pikachu pulled up its tail and flung a
Magikarp at Ash.

Ash tried to grab it, but Magikarp was too slippery.

Its tail slapped Ash in the face!

Then Magikarp flopped back into the sea.

"*Pi. Ka.*" Pikachu shook its head.

"I got one!" Lillie snagged a Milotic.

The Tender Pokémon was beautiful, but strong!

Lillie did not like to touch Pokémon.

Lana and Ash raced to help her.

"Hang on!" called Ash. "We're coming!"
He jumped off his Lapras toward Lillie's.
But the Milotic was quick.
It knocked Ash into the ocean and swam
away.

"Let's take a break," called Professor Kukui.

The Ride Pokémon brought Ash and his classmates to a tiny island.

"Don't leave us, okay?" Ash said to Wailmer and Lapras.

"*Pika, pika!*" Pikachu waved.

Pikachu, Popplio, and Bounsweet raced
across the sand.
It felt good to be back on land!
But they were not safe for long.

"Alola, fair students!" called a voice from above.

Team Rocket hovered above Ash and his friends in their hot-air balloon.

"Heads up, school twerps!" Meowth said.

Meowth dropped a net over the Ride Pokémon.

Then Team Rocket raised the balloon high into the air.

"Dig it, while Meowth takes flight!" he screeched.

"Team Rocket, let's fight!" said Jessie and James.

"*Pika! Pika!*" Pikachu shook a fist at Team Rocket.

"No way!" Ash called. "Get back here!"

Ash and his friends ran after Team Rocket.

But the balloon was too fast!

"Pikachu, let's free the Ride Pokémon into the sea!" Ash said. "Iron Tail. Let's go!"

"*Pi. Ka. Chuuuu!*" Pikachu flung a lightning bolt at Team Rocket.

Their net broke. The Ride Pokémon fell toward the crashing waves!

"*Pika!*" cried Pikachu.

The Ride Pokémon were going to land on the rocks!

Lana and Popplio stepped up.

"Popplio, let's do this!" Lana said.

"*Pop. Plio!*" The Sea Lion Pokémon dove
into the water.

Then it darted up into the air.

It blew the biggest water balloon ever!

"Man, that's a huge balloon!" said Ash.

"Launch the water balloon," called Lana. Popplio let go of its balloon just as the Ride Pokémon were about to hit the rocks. Lapras and Wailmer bounced off the bubble. They landed in the water with a big splash.

"Popplio, we did it!" shouted Lana.

"*Popplio!*" The little Pokémon clapped its flippers.

"That was great!" Ash cheered.

"*Pika!*" Pikachu agreed.

But the battle was not over yet.
Team Rocket called on their Mimikyu.
"Use Shadow Ball!" they commanded.

Mimikyu hurled a black blob at the Ride Pokémon.

"Popplio, use Balloon!" Lana called.

Popplio blew a new water balloon.

Mimikyu's attack bounced against the balloon—and right back at Team Rocket!

"Rowlet, Leafage!" called Ash.
Rowlet's wings turned green.
It blasted Team Rocket with sharp,
glowing leaves.

Pop! Team Rocket's hot-air balloon exploded. Jessie, James, and Meowth dropped toward the sea.

Before they hit bottom, Bewear caught them.

"We're off with a new plan!" Team Rocket cried as Bewear carried them away.

"I'm so glad you're okay," Lana told the Ride Pokémon.

"You and Popplio are lifesavers," Ash told Lana.

"*Pika!*" Pikachu agreed.